FOR ED AND TOM

RED FOX

UK | USA | Canada | Ireland | Australia | India | New Zealand | South Africa

Red Fox is part of the Penguin Random House group of companies
whose addresses can be found at global.penguinrandomhouse.com.

www.penguin.co.uk   www.puffin.co.uk   www.ladybird.co.uk

 Penguin
Random House
UK

First published by The Bodley Head Ltd 1979
This Red Fox edition published 2017
001
Copyright © Shirley Hughes, 1979

The moral right of the author has been asserted

Printed in China

A CIP catalogue record for this book is available from the British Library

ISBN: 978-1-782-95735-5

All correspondence to:
Red Fox, Penguin Random House Children's, 80 Strand, London WC2R 0RL

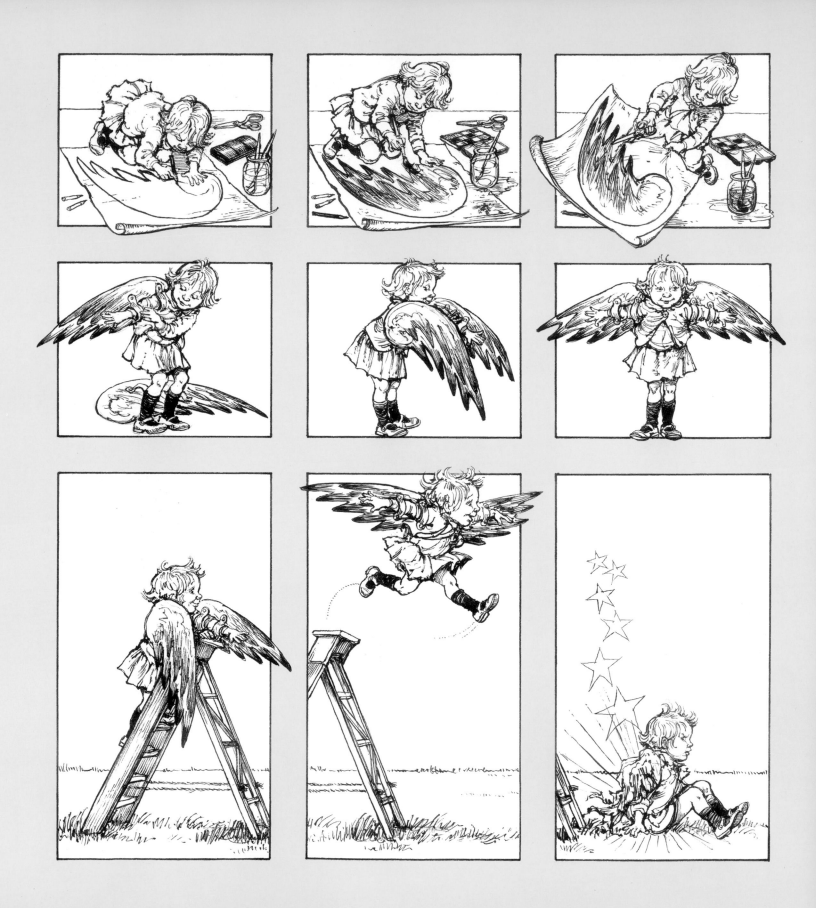

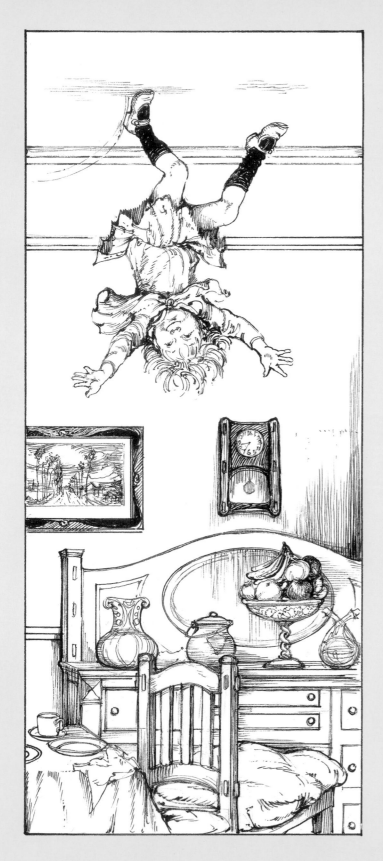

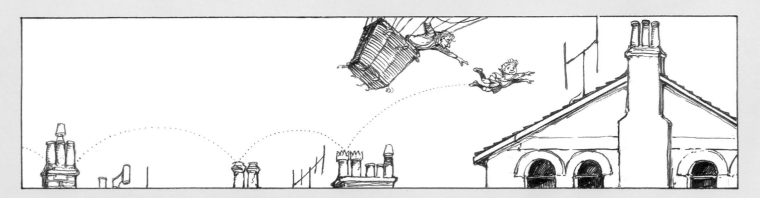

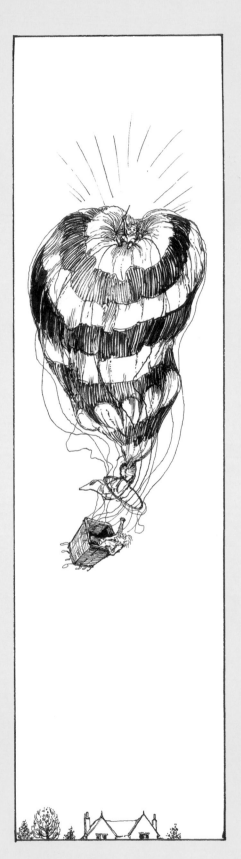